April's Showe

By: Sharon Lopez

This is a work of fiction. Similarities to real people, places, or events are entirely coincidental.

APRIL'S SHOWERS

First edition. April 12, 2024.

ISBN: 979-8215524084

Written by Sharon Lopez.

Chapter 1

April didn't know what made her such an easy target. She wasn't your typical loner with no friends. In fact, the opposite was true. She just didn't interact with them outside of school. It started small at first, a few laughs when she passed, or a mean word or two. Soon, it escalated to trips while walking to art or the library, missing lunch boxes...

"Yes, missing lunch boxes. That isn't all they did. That isn't the point. Do you want to hear this? I could easily stop the conversation. You asked to hear this, and this is where it all began."

April followed her classmates as they made their way to the school's library. Today's story would be Charlotte's Web, one of her favorites. She was next in line to find her seat. After taking a few steps, she lost her footing. She grasped for anything to slow her fall, but all she caught was air. She landed hard on her knees and palms. Peering back, she noticed Wes's leg outstretched, a smirk planted firmly on his face. She tried to will the tears not to fall as the throbbing started in her knees. As laughter filled the air, she felt the drop roll down her cheek.

Not again, she moaned to herself.

The teacher, Mrs. Bower, rushed over and kneeled in front of April. "Are you all right, dear?"

April gave a nod as she felt another droplet land on the top of her hand.

Mrs. Bower helped April to her feet. Her eyes widened for a moment, and then she turned toward her class. "Jenny, bring April to the nurse's office, please."

"I'm okay, I don't need..." April winced as she took a step forward. She glanced down at her knees and let out a small gasp. Her tights bore small red stains in the center of each knee.

As the pout formed, Mrs. Bower jumped into action. She motioned for her aide to tend to the children and then gave her attention to April. "April, what's your favorite candy flavor?"

She stopped before fresh tears spilled over. "W ... what?"

The teacher stooped and leaned in toward April. "Mrs. Gilbert has a bowl of hard candies on her desk," she whispered.

April's eyes lit up. "Really?"

Mrs. Bower nodded with a smile. "And I bet if we ask her nicely, she would share some with you."

"Do you think so?"

The teacher stood and held out her hand. April took it, and the pair set off to find the librarian.

Mrs. Gilbert opened the door wide, noticing April and her teacher standing there, inviting them in with a wide grin. "Hello, April. Mrs. Bower. What brings you to see me?"

"April had a bit of a fall and I thought we would stop by on our way to the nurse's office."

"Hm, is that so? Well, I'm very sorry for the reason you came, but I have some exciting news that will cheer you right up."

"What is it?"

"Well, today is two fer Tuesday."

"Wow, what's that?"

Mrs. Gilbert turned from left to right, her eyes sweeping the room with a theatrical flair. "That means you get to pick two candies from my bowl."

"Two? Just for me?"

Mrs. Gilbert giggled at the girl's excitement. "Yes, all for you. Help yourself."

Approaching the desk, April's eyes were drawn to the assortment in front of her. She eagerly grabbed a bright red one from the bowl, quickly unwrapped it, and popped it into her mouth. The bright orange candy caught April's eye, and she snatched it up before shoving it into her pocket. With a slight slurping sound and a puffed-out cheek, she made her way back towards the teachers. "Thank you, Mrs. Gilbert."

The Librarian smiled and patted the girl's head. "You are very welcome, April."

Mrs. Bower led her out of the office and toward the nurse.

April was disappointed to find that story time had already ended when she arrived back at the library. After giving her pass to Mrs. Gilbert, she took her place in the line with her classmates.

"Did you have a nice trip?" She heard Wes ask in a deep whisper.

"Yeah, see you next fall," Patrick finished in the same tone.

Several children giggled.

April's exhale was shaky, and she braced herself for a hard day ahead.

April was certain that she had placed her lunchbox in the class bin, yet she could not find it during lunchtime the following day. She felt a tap on her shoulder and turned around to see a lunch room monitor standing behind her.

"Is everything okay?"

April scowled, shaking her head. "My lunch box is missing."

The man peered around April, studying the bin. "Are you sure you put it in there?"

"Yes."

"Well, let's go get you a bagged lunch for now. You can ask your teacher about it when you get back to class."

April kicked at the floor. Bagged lunches were gross.

The person who made the sandwiches didn't seem to care that she preferred them cut in half with the crusts off. They were clueless about the unique jelly trick her mother used to spread the jelly evenly on the bread.

She dragged her feet towards the front of the room, already dreading the embarrassment of being the only one without lunch.

After picking at her lunch, April discarded the rest and stepped out into the warmth of the midday sun.

On her way to the playground, she noticed a piece of red plastic glinting in the sunlight on the sidewalk. As she approached, she noticed a larger piece just a few steps ahead. She stooped to get a closer look and saw that her name was written in her mother's favorite green sharpie. Why would her name be on a piece of red ... the *top to my thermos!* Upon jumping to her feet, April began searching for more pieces. She found the rest of her thermos in a nearby bush and later found the top cover of her lunchbox at the end of the path. She carefully gathered the broken pieces and took them to the duty aid, who instructed her to inform her teacher when she got back to class. April frowned, sitting outside her classroom until Mrs. Bower opened the door.

"April, what on earth...? Is that your lunchbox?"

April felt a tear slide down her face as she nodded.

"What happened to it?"

"I don't know. It wasn't in the bin, so I had to eat a bagged lunch. When I came outside, I found pieces everywhere."

Mrs. Bower pursed her lips. "Jenny, bring the children in and start lesson three. April and I are going to the office."

April returned to class, minus the armful of pieces she once held. Her cheeks heated as she returned the stares of her classmates. After handing the teacher her pass, she sat down in silence. Before continuing her lesson, Mrs. Bower offered April a small, reassuring smile.

"For crying out loud, Lois, what do you want me to do? If I don't use my tools, I can't make money."

"Why don't you use them on your job site?"

"I can't lug a 350-pound machine back and forth to work."

April huddled under her blankets, listening to the muffled sounds of her parents' argument.

"Think of something. The electric bill is outrageous!"

"You have always handled the bills; you figure it out!"

Tucking herself in tighter, April let out a low whine.

April followed Trina. Their hushed whispers filled the air with excitement about the new Saturday cartoons. Trina was quick to react when April tripped, preventing her from hitting the ground.

"Jerks," she whispered under her breath, her voice filled with anger. "Are you okay, April?"

April nodded, giving her friend a faint smile.

Trina and April's friendship flourished after Trina's transfer to the school, but April was met with the increased frequency of bullying. Their harassment escalated over time, becoming more severe.

As soon as April entered the bathroom, she felt a sudden push from behind that sent her tumbling onto the frigid floor. The sound of giggling grew louder as someone raised her foot. April was startled when she felt a tug on her shoe, followed by a cool breeze on her foot. Hearing the bathroom door shut, she stood up. Peering downward, she realized a shoe was missing, and the tights she wore had a tear in the leg. Taking a deep breath to calm herself, she limped towards the office.

After listening to her retelling, the principal sent her to the nurse's office to call home. The thought of calling her mother at work made her anxious. Just as she was about to hang up, her father's rough voice echoed through the phone.

"Dad?" The word caught in April's throat, causing her to choke on a sob.

Ms. Jagels, the nurse, held out her hand.

With a tear streaking down her cheek, April handed her the phone.

She sighed, her heart heavy as she listened to the nurse explain the situation to her father.

Once she hung up, Ms. Jagels patted her knee. "There, there."

April cried at the woman's kind gesture.

"Oh now, it will be all right, dear."

April's tears streamed down her face as Ms. Jagels tried to console her, her hand moving in a steady rhythm on her back.

April's father didn't just bring her another pair of shoes; he signed her out for the rest of the day. She was quiet on the drive home, her mind racing as she braced herself for her father's reaction.

"So, how long has this been going on?"

April's eyes flicked up to her dad's face before dropping to her lap.

"I can't help ya, kid, if you don't talk to me."

She sniffled.

He sighed and ruffled the hair on top of her head. The calluses on his hands provided a sense of protection, making her feel safe for the first time in days. Her mother's reaction was not as compassionate.

"You can't just take her out of school every time someone looks at her cross-eyed!"

"They pushed her down and stole her shoe, for God's sake!"

"Harmless pranks. She needs to be tougher and they will stop picking on her."

"You didn't see her. She's miserable."

"She has to go to school. Her education is more important than some silly kids."

Her father sighed, signaling the end of her parents' conversation. Hearing his footsteps coming down the hall, she turned over and closed her eyes. Her bedroom door creaked open, and she felt the soft touch of her dad tucking her blanket around her. His footsteps retreated and then paused.

"Damn it," her father whispered before shutting her door.

The sound of April's laughter mixed with the creaking of the swing as Trina told her a silly joke.

"Hey April!"

As April turned, a sharp object flew into her eye. Her eye stung fiercely, causing her to squint and wince. As she hit the ground with a thud, she let out a cry, covering her face with both hands.

"Ow!"

"April, what happened?"

"Something hit me in the eye."

"I'll be right back. Try not to rub it."

Running as fast as she could, Trin left to find the nurse and their teacher. A few minutes later, she returned to find a curious crowd had gathered around April.

Mrs. Bower, accompanied by the nurse and Trina following behind, navigated through the throng of children.

"Pardon me."

"Excuse me."

"Let us through!"

Trina's outburst was met with disapproving head shakes from the women.

Ms. Jagels stooped in front of April. "Can you move your hands, April? I need to see your eye."

With the whispering crowd in the background, April became uncooperative.

"Mrs. Bower, could you do something about the..." Ms. Jagels motioned toward the students.

"Time to line up."

"The bell didn't ring," one student groaned.

"We want to see what happened," moaned another.

The sound of the ringing bell was music to everyone's ears, but the children groaned in unison as they left one by one.

"Can I stay with April?"

"I'm afraid not, Trina."

She pouted, hugging April tight. "Feel better."

April sniffled.

"Can you stand, dear?"

April nodded.

Mrs. Bower and Ms. Jagels each took one of April's arms, supporting her as they walked towards the nurse's office. After an examination and another call to her father, April cried bitterly, feeling as if the bullies had won again.

"What happened?"

"D ... dad." April barely made out the word before breaking down again.

"This really has to stop. My daughter isn't safe here."

Mrs. Bower's face was grim. "I wish I could disagree with you, but too much has happened. April, do you have any idea who is doing these things to you?"

April raised her head, squinting through the blurred vision caused by the stinging in her eye. She thought about Adam, Patrick, Shawn, and Wes. She remembered how everyone, from teachers to kids, adored them. As a quiet, introverted girl, she knew her story would be dismissed in favor of the popular kids' version.

She said nothing, choosing to shrug her shoulders.

April's dad sighed in frustration.

Mrs. Bower pouted. "Without a name, the best we can do is keep a closer watch over her."

"You mean she has to continue to be bullied until you figure out who is doing this to her?"

"Mr. Richards, I know all of this is frustrating—"

"Frustrating? I passed frustrated months ago! I am furious that my daughter is being terrorized and no one will lift a finger to help her. Seriously, look at her!"

April's lip quivered. Leaping from her seat, she ran into the door frame on her way out of the room. Her father's desperate pleas for her to stop followed her as she ran down the halls. She let out a low grunt as she slammed her palms against the heavy school doors, then pushed with all her might. With a little effort, she managed to push the door open just a crack, enough to squeeze through. Her shoes slapping against the sidewalk.

Gasping for air, she stumbled forward, tears, and snot streaming down her face. The side walk gave way to soft dirt as she reached the park entrance. She made her way to the only spot that she knew was safe.

Behind the tall maple tree's shade, at the far end of the playground, stood the round structure. Metal, peeling paint, and nearly forgotten by the world, stood her hideaway. It would have still looked like a turtle if the eyes that were once painted on hadn't worn off years ago.

She squeezed through the small opening, scooting as far back as she could manage. There she wheezed, coughed and wiped her face dry as she sheltered herself from the day's events.

If she acted more like the other girls, this wouldn't be happening. If she wore dresses and pig tails no one would give her an extra thought. Her mother's words echoed in her head.

That wasn't April. April enjoyed digging in the mud and playing kickball. Jeans and T-shirts were her go-to outfits, and she detested anything as restrictive as a dress. She kept her beloved green and black tennis shoes within reach, while banishing the little white dress shoes with the ankle-digging buckle to the depths under her bed. She remembered how upset her mother was when she had lost them, vowing to never get her another pair until she found the white torture devices. That was fine. She never wanted the first ones to begin with.

April's breathing returned to normal. Her tears stopped. Closing her eyes, she leaned against the cool metal.

After some time, she heard her name being called and opened her eyes. She squinted; someone assaulted her eyes with a bright light.

"H ... Hello?"

"April?

"Dad!" April scurried out and threw her arms around her father.

"I was so worried about you."

"Sorry I ran off."

"I'm sorry too. I was just trying to help."

April widened her uninjured eye.

"We've been searching everywhere for you."

Why is it so dark? Did I fall asleep?

"I didn't have time to make dinner. We'll have to stop—"

"We won't stop anywhere. She can go to bed without dinner for what she pulled!"

April swallowed hard. "Mom."

"Mom? Is that all you have to say for running off and making everyone worry about you?" Mrs. Richards stormed up to April and smacked her in the face.

"Hey, there's no need—"

"No need! Do you realize we had to get the police involved? The police! We'll be lucky if they don't get DCS involved!"

"Linda, you're overreacting."

Mrs. Richards stomped her foot and then turned on her heel. "We're leaving. Let's go!"

Mr. Richards cuddled April to his side. "Are you alright?"

April nodded as fresh tears fell from her eyes.

Her dad sighed. "Let's go home."

That night, April went to bed without dinner, as her mother had predicted. She tossed and turned, finally pressing her pillow over her head to drown out her mother's ear-piercing screeches and her father's failed attempts to make her mother see the truth.

School the next day did not help April's mood. Her father's pleas to keep her home fell on deaf ears. She would have to endure the day's torture on top of the pain her swollen eye was providing.

"Oh, that looks painful."

April peered up from her PB&J to find Wes's smirking face invading her much-needed personal space. She sighed, taking a nibble from her sandwich.

"I wonder who did that?"

April cringed hearing Shawn behind her.

"Yes, someone should do something about it," added Adam.

"They should," Patrick whispered in her ear.

April tried to swallow, but choked instead.

"Let me help you." Patrick picked up April's water bottle and held it out to her.

When she reached for it, he let go, causing it to fall, splattering water over her lap.

The boys laughed as tears filled her eyes.

April ran from the lunchroom, not stopping until she reached the nurse's office. Ms. Jagels glanced up at her from her desk, pointing to a drawer. April opened it. Her father had indeed brought some shoes and changes of clothes, as he promised he would, including pants she could use in cases like today. She pulled a pair of pants from the pile, heading to Ms. Jagels' bathroom to change. She smiled when she found a Hershey's Kiss in the pocket.

After some encouraging words from Ms. Jagels and the sweet, chocolaty treat, April set off for the playground. The boys snickered as she passed. Her shoulders sank, but she continued on until she reached the swings.

Trina grinned as April took a seat on the swing next to her. "I'm sorry I missed lunch. I had a doctor's appointment this morning. Were they horrible?"

April wiped at her uninjured eye. "The worst."

Trina scowled toward the bullies. "There must be something we can do."

"It will only make it worse."

"I think they are getting worse all on their own." Trina stood; her small fists planted on her hips.

April grabbed for her friend's arm but caught only air. "What are you doing?"

"Something!"

Trina stomped to some older boys playing basketball. She yelled, her hands and fingers flailing. When she halted and signaled in her direction, April shuddered. She gasped when Trina pointed to her tormentors. April didn't notice her hands trembling as she watched the group of older boys confront the bullies. Her eyes widened as the taller boy grabbed Wes by his shirt. He twisted and pulled out of the older boy's grasp before he could punch him. The bullies ran off the court and out of sight while Trina jumped up and down with her fist high in the air. April felt nauseous. The bullies would not let this go unpunished. She let out a giant sigh and dug the toe of her shoe into the sand.

Punishment descended while she was at P.E. the next day. 'Someone' stole her clothes from her locker, making another trip to the special drawer in the nurses' office necessary. Her treat this time was a snack sized candy bar.

After school, a crowd of kids gathered together. Curious, April made her way through the crowd. To her dread and the rest of the school's delight, flying high on the flagpole, flew her stolen outfit. The janitor was searching for the key for the lock while two teachers were struggling to break up the throng of laughing children.

That afternoon, April's father met her when she stepped through the door after school. His eyes were filled with sadness.

"I have to go away for a while."

"Where are you going?"

"Your mom and I just need some time apart."

"I want to go with you!"

"I would love that too, but you have to stay here for now."

Tears streamed down April's face. "But I want to go with you, daddy."

Mr. Richards' heart broke knowing he had to leave April behind. Picking her up, he hugged her tight. His eyes filled with tears. He would do his best to fight for custody of her. He hoped she would understand someday.

Chapter 2

"How could you say that?" Shawn fake cried as he entered the classroom.

April rolled her eyes, sitting at her desk.

Shawn theatrically sunk to his knees on the floor to the right and slightly behind her. "You know how much I love you!"

"Go screw yourself, Shawn!" April groaned, pulling her things from her backpack.

The now seventh grade bullies had a new game, and this was it. While Shawn 'poured his heart out' to April, his friends whispered amongst themselves about how she must have led him on.

Two weeks prior, much to her horror, April's science teacher, unaware of the situation, interrogated her in front of the entire class. He asked how she felt about Shawn, since his feelings for her were crystal clear. When she boldly told the teacher she hated him, Shawn sobbed fake tears, and the class erupted in boos and whispers.

The once-friendly faces of her science classmates now glared at April, thanks to the bullies' manipulations. They were diligently working hard to do the same in her history class.

Their menacing behavior had been going on for five years now, and April loathed having to go to school every day.

Her father, who was once her constant rescuer, had grown exhausted of her mother and moved from the house a few years earlier.

Her mother, convincing the judge that she was better equipped to handle the day-to-day things with a few well-placed fake tears, received most of the custody with weekend visitation going to her father.

This left April open to the bullies' attacks during the week, with no one to help put a stop to it. April was at wit's end between the bullies, her science classmates, and her mother, who had become intolerable since her father's departure. So she began skipping class to find a moment's peace.

April slipped from her back yard hiding place after her mother left for work, same as she had been doing for weeks. She marched to the back door and tried to turn the handle. Locked.

Wait, what? "Why is the door locked?" April's heart pounded a little harder. She had her key to the front door, but ... Mrs. Pruitt. The little old lady next door. If she were to see her, her mother would find out she wasn't at school.

April let out a ragged breath and ran her hand through her hair. She tiptoed up to the gate, gingerly lifting the latch. She closed it without making a sound. Turning around, she was met by a wagging tail.

"H ... hi, Henry. Good dog. Go home ... quietly." April waved her hand, shooing Mrs. Pruitt's Pomeranian.

It all seemed to happen in slow motion. Henry playful yipped. April made a sudden movement toward the dog, trying to shush it before her neighbor heard. Henry jumped back and barked.

"Henry?"

Oh god, Mrs. Pruitt! April rushed back to the gate and swung it open. Before she could close it, Henry bounded in after her, yelping as if it were playtime.

April ducked behind a tree.

"Henry ... naughty dog. Come out of there," Mrs. Pruitt stepped through the gate. "Are you chasing that stray cat again?" Mrs. Pruitt made her way to Henry and the tree. Crouching to pick him up, she saw April hiding. "April? What on earth are you doing home, dear?"

April stood, wiping dirt from her jeans. "I wasn't feeling very well, Mrs. Pruitt. I tried to open the back door, but Mom must have locked it."

"Why didn't you go in through the front?"

"I ... I forgot my key when I left this morning."

"Oh, you poor dear. Come, rest at my house until your mom gets home. I'll make you some soup. That will have you feeling better in no time."

April giggled nervously. "Thanks, Mrs. Pruitt."

I could lie down for a bit and then sneak back before my mom comes home, she thought. When her mother asked her about it later, she could just pretend not to know what she was talking about.

She followed Mrs. Pruitt back through the gate. Her mother, who had forgotten something, sealed her fate with the slamming of her car door.

"Mrs. Pruitt? A ... April? What are you doing here?"

"Mom."

"Hello, Linda. Henry gave April a fright. She isn't feeling well. I was just taking her home to rest for a while."

"Really? You seemed fine when you left. Thank you, Mrs. Pruitt, I'll get her to bed."

Mrs. Pruitt patted April's arm. "Feel better, dear."

After slamming the door behind them, April's mother started in. "Why are you really home?"

"I don't feel well."

"Don't lie to me, April. You were fine before you left."

Knowing what, or rather who, waited for April at school made her feel sick to her stomach. Technically, she wasn't lying.

The telephone rang. April's mom answered.

"Yes, this is Ms. Richards. Yes, I am with her now. She said she isn't feeling well. What? The other days? How many other ... Over a month?! And you are just now letting me know? Of course, I didn't know! No, I did not excuse them! Yes, I will be in later to see the principal. Goodbye."

Ms. Richards turned on her heel. She moved quicker than April could respond. She slapped her across the face, car keys still in hand. They dug into April's skin, leaving behind a slight cut.

April scowled, holding her face.

"You're grounded! For one month!"

"A month?"

"Yes, a day for everyday you skipped school."

April rolled her eyes. "Whatever."

Later that afternoon, Ms. Richards and April went to see the principal. April received a week's worth of in school detention.

An entire week without the bullies was a gift, not a punishment, and her mother caught on to April's newfound happiness.

"I think I need to add some more chores to your list."

"Why?"

"You seem so happy. What lesson are you learning?"

"I won't skip school anymore."

"How do I know that?"

"I already told you I wasn't going to."

"How can I trust you after what you did? You're probably lying."

April sighed as she continued to mop the floor.

Chapter 3

April knocked on the door. She was expecting her friend John to answer, but that's not who answered the door.

"Oh, my god."

April's eyes widened.

John stepped in front of Adam, eyeing him as he passed. "Sorry about my brother. He was just leaving."

"Your brother?"

John usually went to April and Trina's. This was the first time she had been to John's house. She did not realize they were related. Two brothers that were so different living in the same house. It took everything for April to stand there.

Adam's glare stayed on April. "Seriously? What the hell are you doing here?"

"Actually, I invited her. I didn't realize you two knew each other," John said, closing the door after April.

April snapped out of her shock at seeing one of the bullies. Anger filled her as she made their past known.

"Oh, you could say that. If by knowing each other you mean that your brother and his friends spent years of my school life terrorizing me."

"You've got to be kidding me. Terrorizing? That's what you're calling it?"

"What else would you call four boys bullying me throughout most of my school years?"

"Whatever. I don't have time for this shit." Adam turned to leave.

"Seriously, Adam, you bullied her?"

"Screw off, John. They were harmless little pranks. And that was years ago."

"Don't you have somewhere to be?"

Adam spun around furiously . "Bitch, you don't talk to me like that in my house. If anyone is going to leave..."

"It's you."

Adam turned toward his sister's voice. "Sara, she…"

"Has been a friend of John's for years."

"She's a total sweetheart."

"Fantastic, you too, Melanie?" Adam turned. His jaw clenched. A vein in his forehead bulged against his skin. "You will regret starting this war, April. Mark my words."

John stood in front of April. "Get out, Adam!"

Adam glanced from his sisters to his brother and threw up his hands. Knowing he had lost this argument, he stormed off, slamming the door behind him.

April enjoyed her time with her friend John and his sisters, finally leaving just after five O'clock. She had just enough time to shower and change to be on time to meet her dad at the restaurant.

When she didn't show up, Mr. Richards called her cell phone. He tried her roommate when she didn't answer.

"Mr. Richards. I was just going to call you."

"Is she with you?"

"I'm with her, yes."

"What's wrong? You sound like you've been crying. Is she okay?"

"April's at the hospital."

"What! What happened?"

"It's those guys. The boys from when we were kids."

"The bullies? How do you know?"

"She told me before she lost consciousness."

"Have you called the police?"

"Yes, they are sending an officer to the hospital."

"I'll be there soon, Trina."

"Alright, Mr. Richards."

"And now you know the entire story. I need you to find those horrible men that did this to my daughter. The bullies that assaulted her."

"We will find them, Mr. Richards. As soon as Ms. Davis finishes her statement, my partner and I will join in the manhunt."

"I've told you everything I know."

"Just once more, Ms. Davis. I want to make sure I have it all written correctly."

"April called me from the gas station on her way home. She said she went to see John, and his brother Adam was there."

"Adam was one of these bullies from when April was growing up?"

"Yes. They messed with her for years."

"What made them stop?"

"Honestly? I think it had something to do with Kylan Best."

"Who's Kylan Best?"

"He stood up for April in eighth grade. The bullies had caught April alone between classes. Kylan used that route to his class and came upon the scene. He chased the bullies off."

"Have you kept in touch with him?"

"April did. They became friends after that day. They were pen pals when he shipped off to the army after high school. I know she talked with him over the phone at least once a week after he came back."

"We will get his number from her phone."

"And the bullies' names. Let me see if I have this right. Wes Bray, Patrick Radford, Shawn Chavez, and Adam Jones."

"Yes. That's right."

They rounded the bullies up one by one and brought them in for questioning. Each of them denied knowing anything about the assault on April.

The detectives needed to gather evidence against the bullies. They decided the best course of action was to talk to people that were around them during the incidents. It was time to speak with Kylan Best.

"Mr. Best?"

"It's about time someone came to see me."

"So, you know why we are here?"

"April. Is she ok? I don't know what hospital they took her to and don't have anyone else's number."

"She is stable. She is at Fairbanks Hospital."

"Thank you. I've been frantically calling hospitals, but they wouldn't tell me if she was a patient."

"How did you know she was in the hospital?"

"I figured she would be after what I overheard."

"What did you hear?"

"I was on the phone with her when they attacked her."

"Why didn't you report it?"

"I did. They said they would send someone out to talk to me. No one ever came ... until now."

"We are here now. Please tell us everything you know."

"Come in. It's going to be a long story."

The three men went into the house and sat down.

"I first met April in eighth grade. Some guys had her pinned against a wall. She looked scared. I ran over and punched one of them. They ran away after that. That's when she told me they had been bullying her for years. No one believed her, so the schools did nothing about it."

"We've heard as much from her father and roommate."

"Alright, then I'll skip forward to today. April called me while she was driving. She said she thought she was being followed. She sounded as scared as the day I met her. I told her to stop at a crowded store and I would meet her, but they ran her off the road before she could."

"They?"

"She called them the bullies, but I heard the names Wes, Patrick, Shawn, and Adam once they caught up with her."

"Caught up with her?"

"She got out of her car and ran into the woods. I think she hit the speaker button because I heard footsteps clearly. Someone tripped her, or maybe she fell. Either way, she screamed and a male voice said, get back here..."

"Well, look who we found, Patrick."

"April, it's been far too long. Hasn't it, Wes?"

"It sure has. I couldn't believe when Adam told us you showed up at his house." Wes helped her to her feet.

"His mother's house. I was visiting John."

"Shut up, bitch!" Adam slapped her. "My brother gets a free ride while I help pay that mortgage. It's my house, you got it?"

"Easy Adam. We're just having a conversation."

"You shut up too, Shawn!"

"Hey, what'd I do?"

"You all got slaps on the wrists from your parents that night. I got sent to military school. Military school! You know what they did to me there!"

"We've dealt with them, Adam. They won't hurt you anymore."

"Now we need to deal with her!" Adam pushed April to the ground. She screamed for help.

"Shh, sweetheart. We can't have you breaking up our reunion."

"Get off of me!"

"I said shut up!" Adam kicked her in the side.

April whimpered.

"I thought we were just going to scare her."

"You all agreed to this."

"P ... please don't."

April cried out as another foot kicked her hard in the ribs. Someone yanked her up to her feet by her hair. Fists and feet connected in a frenzied barrage.

"I heard footsteps leave. Everything went silent after that."

"Do you know what night they were referring to?"

"Trina and Mr. Richards went to the bullies' parents when the school wouldn't help. They denied doing anything wrong, but Wes was a known troublemaker. I had heard rumors his dad sent him to military school, believing it would be the discipline he needed."

"Would you know their voices if you heard them again?"

"Yes."

The police brought Kylan to the station. They recorded Wes, Patrick, Adam, and Shawn saying lines used in the attack and then played them for Kylan one by one.

"Yes, yes! They are all a match. They are the ones that attacked April."

"Alright, sit tight, Kylan. Let's see what they have to say now that we have a witness."

The detectives left Kylan and took turns talking to the bullies.

"We wanted to know if you would like to change your story, Mr. Bray?"

"I already told you. I don't know what happened to April."

"Are you sure about that? I have a witness that can place you all at the scene."

"I don't know what your witness..." Wes placed his fingers together to make quotation marks. "Saw, but they didn't see me."

"That's fine. I'm sure the others will take the deal and tell us what really happened."

"What deal?"

"A plea down to aggravated assault."

"Aggravated ... from what?!"

"Attempted murder."

"Attempted murder?!" Wes's eyes went round. "Shit, what happened to her?"

The detective's eyebrow rose. "Is that a serious question?"

"Yeah, I mean, we used to mess with her when we were kids, but attempted murder? What reason would we have to kill her?"

"You're admitting to bullying April Richards?"

"Yes, when we were kids, we all did, but after she set her boyfriend on us, we stopped."

"Her boyfriend?"

"Kylan ... something ... uh ... like great, but not... Best! Yes, Best, that's it."

"Kylan and April were dating?"

"If they weren't, someone needed to tell him that. He went wherever she went, carried her books, walked her to every class, brought her home. I even caught him changing his classes to meet hers."

"What?"

"The guy was completely obsessed with her."

The detective took some notes and then left the room.

"I have nothing more to say to you."

"Calm down, Mr. Radford. I need to ask you about Kylan Best."

"Kylan? What about him?"

"What was his relationship with April Richards?"

"I thought they were a couple. He was infatuated with April."

"But you don't think so anymore?"

"She never liked him like that."

"How do you know that?"

"She told me."

"When?"

"In high school. And..."

"And?"

"About a week ago."

"You saw April a week ago?"

"I ran into her at the grocery store. And by run into I mean, we saw each other and had a conversation."

"She actually talked to a man she refers to as—"

"The bullies? Yeah, I know. She's been calling us that for years. We deserve it, though."

"Why is that?"

"We gave her a hard time when we were kids."

"You bullied her?"

"When I was a kid, I did. It sucked the way we treated her, but I have no reason to beat her up."

"So, what was the conversation that happened between the two of you?"

"I said, Hello..."

"H ... Hi, Patrick."

"How have you been?"

"What do you care?"

"I'm sorry. I didn't mean to upset you."

"You're sorry?" April scoffed.

"Hey, I'm serious. I know I treated you kind of bad when we were kids, but—"

"Kind of bad? You bullied me, Patrick. It wasn't bad, it was hell. Every day for years. I dreaded going to school. I ditched for a month just to get some peace."

"Seriously?"

"Yes."

"Damn. I didn't realize it was that ... That we made you feel like that. I really am sorry."

"Thank you for that."

"So, where's your boyfriend? Is he going to jump out at me from behind the coffee beans?" Patrick peered left and right.

"I don't have one."

"What about that guy from school?"

"Kylan?"

"Yeah."

"We're only friends."

"Really? It seemed like more."

"No, he was like an older brother to me. We've only been friends."

"Oh, it seemed like he was into you."

April shook her head and shrugged.

"And then my girlfriend came over. I introduced the two of them and then we left."

"I will need to talk to her."

"Sure. Do you have a pen? I'll write her name and phone number."

"Mr. Chavez, I was wondering if you could shed some light on something for me?"

"What's that?"

"What do you know about the assault on April Richards?"

"I told the other officer that I know nothing about it."

"If you had to choose someone, that was suspicious. Someone that could want to hurt or scare Ms. Richards. Who would be your first guess?"

"Um, I don't know. Maybe a boyfriend or ex?"

"Does April have one?"

"I haven't talked to her since we were kids."

"Was there anyone that she was dating then?"

"There was one guy that seemed to be around a lot."

"Do you remember his name?"

"I'm not sure. Something with a K. Like Kyle? No, Kylan ... Yeah, that's it, Kylan."

"What was your impression of Kylan?"

"I remember him always being around April. Everywhere she went, he was there too, ya know?"

"Is he the reason you and your friends stopped bullying Ms. Richards?"

"Bullying is a strong word."

"What would you call it?"

"Teas..." Shawn sighed and ran his hand through his hair. "I guess we did bully her. But that was a long time ago."

"And you have had no contact with April Richards since school?"

"No, I haven't. I think the last time I saw her was graduation."

"Did they ever argue?"

"Kylan and April? No, I don't remember any ... wait, now that I'm thinking about it, there was this party one night."

"You saw April Richards and Kylan Best at a party together?"

"They were both there, but I don't think they went to it together."

"Why do you say that?"

"I remember he was pissed at her."

"Kylan was upset with April?"

"Yeah."

"Why?"

"She came with someone else."

"A friend? Another guy?"

"It was another guy. Oh, what was his name? Um, Trevor? Yeah, Trevor Miller."

"Can you tell me what happened?"

"It went something like..."

"Hi, Kylan."

"Hi? April, what are you doing here?"

"Trevor asked me."

"Trevor? You're here with Trevor? Like on a date?"

"No. Not really like a date."

"I thought you didn't date. You were concentrating on your studies?"

"I was ... I am. He just asked and—"

"And you said yes?!"

"What's wrong? Why are you so mad?"

"You know how many times I asked you out? You always told me no."

"I'm sorry, Kylan. I didn't mean to—"

"Whatever. Enjoy your date!" Kylan stormed off.

"Did you ever witness any other arguments between them?"

"No, but..."

"But?"

"When Adam and I left that night, I saw Trevor and Kylan having words."

"They were arguing?"

"I'm not really sure. I only saw them for a second. Adam might know more. He was already outside when I left the house."

"Mr. Jones."

"Look, I'm done sitting here. Either charge me or cut me loose. I've got rights!"

"I apologize for the wait. Can I get you anything? "

"Guess a beer would be out of the question?"

"I could get you water, soda, or coffee."

"I'd love a cup of coffee, actually. Can I smoke?"

The detective pushed the ashtray closer to Adam.

Adam took a pack of cigarettes from his pocket, took one out, lit it, and then placed the pack on the table.

A few seconds later, an officer entered, placing a cup in front of Adam, leaving the way he had entered.

"Yeah, much better," Adam said, exhaling a big puff of smoke.

"You didn't like April Richards much, did you?"

"No, I actually hate the bitch."

"Any reason in particular?"

"Her and her dad. They came to my house and told my parents I was harassing April."

"Weren't you?"

"That's beside the point."

"I think that was the point, Mr. Jones."

"Anyway, like I was saying, they came over and her dad demanded that my parents put a stop to it."

"And did they?"

"Did they ever. The old man shipped me off to military school."

"That must have been hard."

"You do not know the half of it."

"That must have made you angry."

"Damn straight, it did."

"Angry enough to want to hurt April?"

"I wanted that bitch dead!"

"Those are some strong words, Mr. Jones."

"You don't understand. The things that ... What they did."

"What who did?"

"The guys at school."

"What happened?"

"Everyone says I have an attitude."

"You don't say."

"They may have a point, but I haven't had the easiest life."

"What do you mean?"

"My dad and I didn't get along so well."

"Did you fight?"

"It was a little too one-sided to call a fight."

"Are you saying he hit you?"

"More than once."

"So, what happened once you went to military school?"

"Everyone was always so uptight. They reminded me of my dad. I was just trying to get them to lighten up."

"What happened?"

"I drove the Superintendent's car onto the obstacle course. Caused a bit of damage."

"Oof."

"No one would fess up, so we all ended up doing early morning and late-night calisthenics."

"That must have pissed off some people."

Adam swallowed hard. "You could say that."

"Did the boys retaliate?"

"Oh, yeah." Adam reached for his pack of cigarettes, his hand trembling. "A bunch of them came in while I was sleeping." He took a ragged breath and then struggled to light his cigarette. "They took turns holding me down and beating the shit out of me. I ... I was in the hospital for two weeks. My dad was forced to take me home."

"Damn. I could see how that could make you angry."

"You think?! I spent many nights thinking of ways to get back at her."

"Any involve assault?"

"Many ... I even went to her house one night."

"What?!"

"I did nothing. I couldn't. Every time I thought about it, I'd remember..." Adam's words trailed off. He stared into nothingness. His hand was still shaking as bits of ash fell from his cigarette. He sniffled and closed his eyes a few moments later.

"Can you continue?"

"Y ... Yeah." Adam cleared his throat and wiped his eyes.

"Do you remember a party that you and Shawn Chavez went to?"

Adam smirked. The previous emotion vanished. "There were several. You'll have to be more specific."

"One in which there might have been words exchanged between Trevor Miller and Kylan Best?"

"Oh, that party. Yeah, that was one hell of a night."

"What made it stand out?"

"Kylan got in Trevor's face. Trevor waved him off. That pissed off Kylan because he came unglued! He shoved Trevor, which caused him to spill his drink. Trevor turned and decked Kylan."

"What did Kylan do?"

"Nothing."

"Nothing?"

"Nope, he got knocked out. One punch. Bam! Out like a light," Adam laughed.

"Did you see Kylan fight with anyone else?"

"Mm, he was hassling this nerd in the library one day."

"Do you know why?"

"Something about him asking April out."

"This ner..." The detective cleared his throat. "This boy, he asked April out on a date?"

"Yeah. Not sure what his name was. Wes was there. Maybe he knows."

"Mr. Bray, I have another question."

"Shoot."

"Do you remember an altercation between Kylan and another boy inside the library?"

"Oh, you must mean Malcolm."

"Do you know his last name?"

Wes blew out a breath and rubbed his chin. "Young."

"Can you tell me what happened between Mr. Best and Mr. Young?"

"We were all in the library..."

Malcolm stood searching the shelves for a book.

Kylan marched over and grabbed him by the front of his shirt. "You need to stay away from April."

"O ... o... okay."

Kylan released Malcolm and stormed off as fast as he arrived.

"And where exactly are all the teachers when these things are going on? You have a girl being bullied by four boys on multiple occasions, boys being threatened by other boys. From the timeline, I assume this is at a couple of different schools?"

"We picked our spots when the teachers were ... involved with something else or whatever. As far as Kylan, Malcolm was in the back of the library, hidden by bookcases. I only saw him because I was in the area."

"In the area doing what?"

"Copying Malcolm's homework."

The detective blew out a breath in frustration and then left the room. He heard yelling coming from the front of the station. He thought he recognized the voice.

"I heard you have them in custody, Detective Ramirez!"

"Calm down Mr. Richards. We are still questioning them."

"Questioning them? What for? We all know they did it!"

Ramirez motioned for Mr. Richards to follow him. He went into his office and shut the door. "There has been a recent development."

"What does that mean?"

"How well do you know Kylan Best?"

"Kylan? He's been a friend of my daughters for years. He protected her from the bullies."

"Were they ever romantically involved?"

"Not that I'm aware of. What does this have to do with April's attack?"

"We are following all leads, Mr. Richards."

"April told Trina they did it. What more evidence do you need?"

"Has April woken up yet?"

Mr. Richards sighed and shook his head.

"We will keep you informed. Right now, April needs you. Concentrate on your daughter. We will find out who did this to her. Give us some time."

Mr. Richards left. Detective Clark came into their office to compare notes.

"Who do you like for this?"

"After talking with Kylan, I would have sworn it was them."

"But now?"

"They paint quite the picture of Mr. Best. One that can be pretty violent."

"We've got a few people left to talk to."

"Let's talk to this Malcolm Young and Patrick's girlfriend first. See what they can tell us."

"I left a message for Mr. Young, and I already spoke to Ms. Garcia. She's agreed to come down."

"We're running out of room."

Their door opened, and an officer poked his head in. "Jessica Garcia is here."

"Thanks."

"Ms. Garcia, you are dating Patrick Radford?"

"Jessica, and yes, we've been together for almost three years now."

"Do you know April Richards?"

"Patrick introduced us. I know about when they were kids. He told me about it after we got home from the store. It's terrible what they put her through, but they didn't hurt her."

"And how do you know that?"

"We all had plans to go to the game that day. We went back to my home and ordered pizza, too."

"What time did they leave?"

"I'm not sure exactly, but by the time we made it home, it was dark. I could check my receipt."

"We will need you to do that. Do you still have your stubs from the game?"

"I have mine and Patrick's. The boys each had their own."

"They didn't mention being at the stadium. Do you know why that would be?"

"Patrick wouldn't have wanted to involve me in all of this. The boys ... I'm not sure."

"Thank you for coming in, Ms. Garcia. I will have an officer escort you home to collect the stubs and pizza receipt."

"Why wouldn't they tell us they had an alibi?"

"I don't know, Ramirez. Let's go find out."

The two stood to do just that when an officer appeared in the doorway.

"Mr. Young is here."

"Thank you for coming down, Mr. Young."

"You're welcome. What is this about?"

"Do you know Kylan Best?"

"Now there is a name from the past."

"How do you know him?"

"From school. He wanted me to stay away from April Richards."

"Did he say why?"

"No, I was too busy trying not to get punched to ask."

Clark and Ramirez turned, nodding to one another.

Upon hearing of the attack on April, John's mind raced as he hurried towards the police station to see how he could help.

"We understand April came to visit you before the assault."

"Yes. I still can't believe someone did that to her. She's a good person. She doesn't deserve that."

"Was your brother at home when April arrived?"

"Yeah, and I didn't know that they knew each other. It was a shock to learn my brother bullied her."

"Did they talk to one another when she was at your home?"

"Yeah, my brother was a dick!" John cleared his throat. "Sorry. He was rude to her."

"Could you tell us what happened?"

"Yeah, he answered the door and..."

"Oh, my god."

John stepped in front of Adam, eyeing him as he passed. "Sorry about my brother. He was just leaving."

Adam's glare stayed on April. "Seriously? What the hell are you doing here?"

"Actually, I invited her. I didn't realize you two knew each other," John said, closing the door after April.

"Oh, you could say that. If by knowing each other, you mean that your brother and his friends spent years of my school life terrorizing me."

"You've got to be kidding me. Terrorizing? That's what you're calling it?"

"What else would you call four boys bullying me throughout most of my school years?"

"Whatever. I don't have time for this shit." Adam turned to leave.

"Seriously, Adam, you bullied her?"

"Screw off, John. They were harmless little pranks. And that was years ago."

"Don't you have somewhere to be?"

Adam spun around furiously. "Bitch, you don't talk to me like that in my house. If anyone is going to leave..."

"It's you."

Adam turned toward his sister's voice. "Sara, she..."

"Has been a friend of John's for years."

"She's a total sweetheart."

"Fantastic, you too, Melanie?" Adam turned. His jaw clenched. A vein in his forehead bulged against his skin. "You will regret starting this war, April. Mark my words."

John stood in front of April. "Get out, Adam!"

Adam glanced from his sisters to his brother and threw up his hands. Knowing he had lost this argument, he stormed off, slamming the door behind him.

"So, your brother was pretty angry when he left?"

"He was furious when he left."

"Does he behave like that often?"

"He didn't until he came home from military school."

"Thank you for your time, John."

"Of course. Anything to help April."

The detectives moved the bullies into one interrogation room once John left.

"I have a question for all of you."

"When asked for an alibi, none of you mentioned going to a football game and then to Ms. Garcia's for pizza. Why is that?"

The men peered at each other and then back at Detectives Clark and Ramirez.

"I asked them not to mention it."

"Why would you do that, Mr. Radford?"

"I didn't want Jessica involved."

"If each of you can produce your game ticket stubs, it proves your innocence. Why would that be a problem for Ms. Garcia?"

"It's Mrs."

"I see."

"Don't judge; they've been apart over a year."

"I am merely asking a question. Mrs. Garcia has given each of you an alibi. She has also produced your ticket stub and receipt for the pizza, Mr. Radford. You are free to go."

"And for the rest of us?"

"Mr. Bray, Mrs. Garcia gave you an alibi. Your ticket stubs will prove your innocence beyond a reasonable doubt."

Patrick stood. "Jessica got involved. Just give them what they want."

"This way Mr. Radford." Patrick followed Detective Clark out of the room.

Shawn took out his wallet and removed a torn ticket stub. "Here." He handed it to Detective Ramirez and then placed his wallet back in his pocket.

Detective Ramirez motioned for Shawn to follow and led him from the room.

"And then there were two," Detective Clark said, sitting down.

Detective Ramirez leaned against the wall. "Three, if you include Mr. Best."

"I'd almost forgotten about him." Clark rolled his eyes.

"He demanded we feed him lunch if he was going to be kept all day."

Detective Clark laughed. "What did you do?"

"I had Officer Woods bring him coffee and a sandwich from the vending machine."

"What about Adam and Wes's ticket stubs?"

"They said they threw them away."

"Convenient."

"Do we bring Mrs. Garcia back down?"

"She may have lied once to protect those two. I doubt her story would change."

"Wait, do you remember what she said?"

"She said they went to the game and to her house for pizza."

"No, she said, 'We all had plans to go to the game that day. We went back to my home and ordered pizza, too.'"

"Hmm, maybe not everyone showed up?"

"Out of everyone, I would have liked one of them for this." Detective Clark motioned toward the interrogation rooms.

"They are the biggest trouble make ... rs" Detective Ramirez's eyebrow rose. "Wait!" He slapped his notebook on the table and began thumbing through it.

"What is it?"

"Trouble maker ... Kylan. He said Wes was a known troublemaker."

"So?"

"Military school. Wes never went to military school. It was Adam. Yeah, right here. Kylan said Trina and Mr. Richards went to the bullies' parents when the school wouldn't help. They denied doing anything wrong, but Wes was a known troublemaker. I had heard rumors his dad sent him to military school. He said Trina and Mr. Richards went to their homes. Adam told us April had gone to his home with her father."

"That's a pretty big mess up."

"It sure is."

"I think it might be time to have another chat with Mr. Best."

"I think you're right."

"Mr. Best, in your earlier statement, you said Mr. Bray was a known troublemaker."

"Yes."

"You went on to say, that his father had sent him to military school."

"That's right."

"But when speaking with him, he never mentioned military school."

"No?"

"No. On the other hand, Mr. Jones got sent to military school."

"I must have gotten the two confused."

"But in your retelling of the attack, you clearly stated Mr. Jones was angry. You said and I quote, 'You all got slaps on the wrists from your parents that night. I got sent to military school.'"

"See, I had it right."

"But how could you get it wrong and right in the same statement?"

"I told you. I got them confused. The attack is the important thing. Getting those details right is what matters in the end."

"Are you sure who went to see the bullies' parents?"

"What do you mean?"

"You said Trina and Mr. Richards went to see them, but Mr. Jones said Ms. Richards went with her father."

"I just heard they went. I assumed Trina went because she and Mr. Richards have been the ones trying to put a stop to it."

"Do you recall Malcolm Young?"

"No."

"He definitely remembers you."

"Who is that?"

"He said you threatened him."

"I rarely leave my apartment. How could I have threatened him?"

"This wasn't a recent altercation."

"What was this supposed altercation about?"

"April."

"What did you just...?" Kylan stood, clenching his fists.

The detectives stepped back, taking a defensive stance.

Kylan advanced. His eyes were saucer-like. His mouth twisted into a snarl. "Don't you dare say her name!"

"Mr. Best, calm down."

He charged at the detectives. Clark moved to the right. Ramirez dodged left. Clark grabbed Kylan's arms, holding them while Ramirez cuffed him.

"No! She is mine! Do you hear me?! No one will have her! Don't even speak her name!"

"You need to cool off! Some time in a jail cell should do it!"

The detectives led Kylan to a cell as he screamed, trying to wrench himself free.

A policeman escorted a man to Clark and Ramirez's office.

"Hello, Mr.?"

Trevor extended his hand. "Trevor Miller. I was told you had some questions for me."

"Yes, thank you for coming down." Ramirez motioned for Trevor to sit.

"Do you know Kylan Best?"

"Do you mean the guy that got in my face back in school?"

"Could you tell us what happened?"

"I was sitting outside greeting guests when Kylan storms up and gets in my face. His breath smelled like beer, so I dodged him, thinking he was drunk."

"Was he?"

"He had been drinking, but I found out later he wasn't drunk."

"Please continue."

"Like I said, I was greeting my guests, and Kylan got in my face..."

"I heard you invited April here on a date!"

"Go sleep it off." Trevor turned around to talk to some friends.

Kylan grasped Trevor's arm and spun him around to face him. Trevor's cup spilled down the front of his shirt. "We're not done!"

"Hey, that's a new shirt! You're going to pay for that!"

"Make a move!"

Trevor balled his fist. His punch connected with Kylan's jaw. Kylan fell to the ground, motionless.

"Look what you made me do." Trevor turned to his friends. "You guys want to help me get him upstairs?"

The boys picked up Kylan and brought him to Trevor's room. Kylan came to the moment he hit the bed.

"What the hell?!" Kylan scooted back until his back hit the wall.

"Easy, I just brought you here to rest." Trevor motioned for his friends to leave. "Look, I don't know why you're so upset, but I never should have punched you."

Kylan rubbed his jaw. "You're here with April."

"Richards? She tutored me in math. I invited her out as a thank you. She's cool and all, but I don't think she likes me like that."

"You're not trying to—"

Trevor held up his hand. "I've got a game tomorrow. I'm not going to bed with anything besides my pillow tonight."

Kylan ran his hand through his hair. "I'm sorry too."

"Did you tell her how you feel?"

"Huh?"

"A girl doesn't know unless you're straight with her."

Kylan nodded his head.

"Alright, let's go back to the party. We're cool?"

"Yeah, we're good. I think I'm going to head home, though."

"Suit yourself."

"Kylan left after that?"

"I led him out the door myself."

"Do you know of any other altercations Mr. Best might have had?"

"Not that I know of. Honestly, the guy was a loner. It surprised me to see him at my party."

"Thank you for your time, Mr. Miller."

Clark and Ramirez had just sat at their desks when a knock sounded on the door.

"Yeah."

The door opened, and an officer stepped through. "Mr. Richards called. His daughter April woke up."

"That's good news."

"We'll head over to the hospital."

Chapter 4

April was sitting up in bed. Her face was swollen and bruised, her right eye only open a slit, and the left eye, open a touch more, was bloodshot. Her lower lip was split; a fresh bandage crowned her head. She looked awkward with an arm in a sling and a heavy cast on the leg visible outside the sheets.

"We understand you have been through a terrible ordeal, Ms. Richards. We will be as brief as we can."

April sipped from a straw in a cup that Trina was holding.

"Do you have any idea who did this to you?"

"I told you who it was," Trina shouted, slamming the cup on the tray.

"They have an alibi, Ms. Davis."

"Then they are lying."

"There is proof."

"You said the bullies did this, April." Trina said, putting her hand on April's arm.

"N ... no. I said not the bullies."

"If it wasn't them, then who was it?"

"We would like that answer, too."

"I don't know who it was."

"You didn't see their face?"

"No, they were wearing masks."

"Then how do you know it wasn't the bullies?"

"It wasn't their voices."

"How many assailants were there?"

"Three people. Two Assailants."

"What do you mean?"

"One stood leaned against a tree watching."

"Sick bastard!"

Ramirez frowned at Clark's outburst.

"I apologize."

"Don't. You're not wrong. The bullying. The assault. My daughter deserves justice."

"People have hurt her enough," Trina added.

"We'll do everything in our power to catch the perpetrators."

"Is there anything that stood out to you, Ms. Richards? Eye color? Height? Body size? Gender? Race?"

"I could tell they were male by their voices. They were taller than I am, so maybe around 5'10 to 6'. They were average mostly. Some muscle. A bit of an athletic build. That's all I really know. I'm sorry."

"Every bit of information helps. They posted an officer outside your door. If you remember anything else, he can reach us."

At their office, Ramirez spun in his chair to face Clark. "Did you notice they all fit her description?"

"The thought occurred to me."

"What if they all were in on it together?"

"What?!"

"Hear me out. I can't shake Kylan's outburst, and the mix-up between Adam and Wes."

"Don't Kylan and the bullies hate each other?"

"I don't know."

"What's the motive?"

"I did some digging and found out something that no one has mentioned in any of their statements."

"What's that?"

"A death certificate."

"For who?"

"Lucas Richards."

"Who's that?"

"A child that was born and then later died in 2012."

"To who?"

"April Richards."

"We've got them for the assault."

"Yeah, but what if they raped her?"

"Rape?"

"Everyone said she didn't have a boyfriend. How did she get pregnant?"

"They would deserve to be punished for it."

"I'll get Adam and Wes. Feel like grabbing, Mr. Best?"

"So, which one of you is the father?" Ramirez asked, throwing open the interrogation room door.

Wes and Adam peered at each other. Confusion filled their faces.

"No? Did you not know?"

"Maybe I should talk to—"

Detective Clark interrupted as he led Kylan into the room, right on cue.

"What the hell is he doing here?"

"Oh, sorry. Wrong room."

"Hey, while you have him here. What do you know about Lucas, Mr. Best?"

Kylan's gaze fell to the floor, and when he looked up, his face was contorted with anger. "How do you know?"

"All births and deaths are public record."

"What does all of this have to do with April's assault?"

"Like you don't know!" Kylan lunged at Adam and Wes. He punched Adam and then kicked Wes upside his head.

"Whoa, whoa, whoa." Detective Ramirez grabbed Kylan and led him out of the room.

"Anyone want to tell me what that was about?" Clark asked, blowing out a deep breath.

Adam rubbed his face. "No idea."

Wes shook his head.

"I said calm down!" Ramirez forced Kylan into a chair. "You want to tell me what that was about?"

"It doesn't matter. You won't do anything about it. Nothing ever happens to them!"

"Tell me."

"They raped her."

"Who?"

"Wes and Adam."

"Why isn't there a report in the system?"

"Because there wasn't one filed."

"Why?"

"For the same reason, April stopped talking about the bullying. No one believed her!"

"Are you saying it continued after your altercation with them?"

"It stopped for a while, but then Wes and Adam started again."

"Why didn't you tell us this before?"

"And what good would it have done?"

"We can't do anything about their bullying, but there's no statute of limitations for rape."

"How do we prove it?"

"You let me worry about that."

Ramirez burst into the room. "You were right, Clark."

"About?"

"The bullying didn't stop. These two kept it going."

"We didn't—"

Adam stood. "You can't prove shit! Besides, we were kids. There isn't anything you can do about it."

Ramirez crossed the room. Mere inches from Adam. "But we can do something about rape."

Adam smirked. "I don't know what you're talking about."

"We will have proof soon enough."

Wes peered around Adam. "What do you mean?"

"April woke up. She told us what happened."

"She's lying."

"You know what doesn't lie? DNA. See, April stopped talking about the bullying, but the one thing she did right was keep her clothes from that night."

Adam slumped into the chair.

"And when we match that DNA to you..."

Wes' eyes went round, and then he glanced at Adam.

Clark and Ramirez left Adam and Wes and went back to their office.

Clark slumped down onto the corner of his desk. "She never told us about the rape."

"Nope."

"There is no DNA evidence."

"Not exactly true."

"What do you mean?"

"If we need it ... Lucas..."

Clark sighed.

Clark and Ramirez made their way to the hospital to speak with April regarding Kylan's statement.

"Mr. Richards, Ms. Davis, can we have a moment alone with Ms. Richards?"

Trina squeezed April's hand. Mr. Richards kissed his daughter's forehead. The two left the room.

"How did you find out?"

The detectives glanced at each other.

"I had a feeling you knew. Why else would you make them leave?"

"Kylan."

April exhaled hard. "He's the only one that knows."

"How did you keep it a secret from your parents?"

"I stayed with Kylan for a couple of years. I just couldn't handle my mom anymore. She never would've let me stay with my dad, so I ran away. It happened during that time."

"The police would've believed you."

"Do you believe me?"

Detective Ramirez nodded.

"What happens now?"

"They took a plea deal so you won't have to testify."

"Between us, the assault, was it them?"

April nodded.

"I know it's hard, but can you tell us what happened?"

"I got out of my car and ran into the woods. Someone tripped me, and I fell. I screamed and Adam said, get back here..."

"Well, look who we found, Wes."

"April, it's been far too long, hasn't it?

"I couldn't believe it when you showed up at my house."

Wes helped her to her feet.

"Your mother's house. I was visiting John."

"Shut up, bitch!" Adam slapped her. "My brother gets a free ride while I help pay that mortgage. It's my house, you got it?"

"Easy Adam. We're just having a conversation. We have to get to the game."

"You shut up too, Wes!"

"Hey, what'd I do?"

"You all got slaps on the wrists from your parents. I got sent to military school. Military school! You know what they did to me there!"

"We've dealt with them, Adam. They won't hurt you anymore."

"Besides, what we did. She can ID us. We need to deal with her before she tells someone!"

"It's been years. The statute of limitations—"

"I read about a case in the paper. There isn't one. We can still do time, even after all these years." Adam pushed April to the ground.

She screamed for help.

"Shh, sweetheart. We can't have you breaking up our reunion."

"Get off of me!"

"I said shut up!"

"P ... please don't do this."

April cried out as a foot kicked her hard in the ribs. Wes yanked her up to her feet by her hair. Fists and feet connected in a frenzied barrage.

"The footsteps left. I laid there half out of it for a while. I pulled my phone from my pocket and called Trina. We have a 'find my phone' app."

"Trina was right, you said, the bullies, when she asked you who did it."

"Yes. No one has done anything to stop them. All these years..." April sniffled.

"I'd like to discuss one more thing."

"What?"

"Kylan Best."

Chapter 5

"You got them for the assault. Why am I here again?"

"We went to see Ms. Richards again, Mr. Best. She confirmed what happened to her."

"It was very similar to your statement."

"I told you I was on the phone with her."

"Yes, you said that."

"There are just a couple of problems with that."

"And what's that?"

"She said she pulled her phone from her pocket to call Trina."

"She was never on the phone during her attack."

"In fact, the two of you haven't spoken since she moved out of your house a couple of years ago."

"No, no, that's not right. I see her all the time."

"That's because you've been stalking her. Isn't that right, Mr. Best?"

"No!"

"April got sick of you scaring away the guys who asked her out."

"Don't say her name."

"So, April moved out and told you to stay away from her."

"That's not true! I love her! She would never ... Ugh!" Kylan lunged at the detectives, but they were ready for him.

Clark held him against the wall, and Ramirez cuffed him. They put him back in the chair and bound him to the table with the handcuffs.

"You were angry with her for moving out."

"If you couldn't have her, no one would, right?"

"You followed her from her friend's house. You were planning to teach her a lesson."

"But someone got there before you did."

"You witnessed her assault. You watched it happen and did nothing!"

"Despite claiming to love her, you watched as two men assaulted her."

"How could you do that?!"

"I loved her! She didn't care. She thought of me as her brother. Her brother! Can you believe that? After everything I did for her, she just left me like she was too good for me!"

"So, she deserved to be beaten?"

"Yes! Whenever she needed someone, I was always the first to be there for her. I offered her a safe place away from her mother, but then she got pregnant with her bastard son! She deserved that beating and more!"

"You never reported it."

"You covered your own ass by telling us what happened."

"Kylan, you're sick."

"And we've got you on stalking, intent to commit a crime, and 2 counts of attempted assault on a police officer."

"You said it yourself, I'm sick ... no judge will find me competent to stand trial."

"You're sick, and I don't care if you spend the rest of your life in jail or in an asylum."

Clark leaned in close to Kylan. "You won't go near April ever again."

Kylan snarled and head-butted Clark.

"Ah!" Clark grabbed his head.

"You, ok?"

"Yeah." Clark laughed.

"What's so funny?"

"He actually assaulted a police officer this time."

"He did. We'll add that, along with resisting arrest, to the list of charges."

"Kylan Best, you're under arrest."

"We have a plea hearing to attend."

"April will not like it."

"Hopefully, we're in time."

"Your Honor, as you can see, the defendants have no priors against them, so we ask that you allow the terms of the plea agreement."

"I wouldn't be so sure about that!"

"I'm sorry, detectives. Do you have something to add to this sentence hearing?"

"We have a lot to add, your honor."

The judge motioned for Clark and Ramirez to come forward.

"Your Honor, I haven't had time to prepare for these new witnesses."

The judge raised his hand. "If you give them a few minutes, we'll all know what's so important that they disrupted this hearing."

Clark and Ramirez glanced at each other.

"We apologize, Your Honor. What we have has direct bearing on this case."

"We have learned of a prior crime—"

"Alleged..." the defense attorney scolded.

"We can more than prove it!"

"Until a guilty verdict—"

"Are you three quite finished?"

"Sorry, Your Honor."

"I apologize, Your Honor."

"How is this crime connected to this case?"

"It's an aggravated sexual assault committed by the defendants against the same victim, Your Honor."

"A—"

"Alleged," Detective Clark added before the defense attorney could finish.

"And you didn't know of this, Mrs. Altman?"

"No, your Honor."

"And the defense had no prior knowledge?"

"No, Your Honor."

"Is the victim willing to come forward?"

"Yes, Your Honor."

"I hereby deny the plea agreement and order the defendants to stand trial for both alleged assault charges."

Wes' and Adam's heads fell into their hands at the judge's decision.

With the knowledge of the upcoming court hearing for the sexual assault, the detectives realized they needed to persuade April to testify.

"You said I wouldn't have to testify!"

"That was before we learned about the sexual assault, Ms. Richards."

"I know this is a lot to take in after everything you've been through—"

"Yes, what I've been through. The years of torment, the ... the... Do you understand Kylan was the only one that knew about the r..."

"Sexual assault?"

"Yes, and the birth of Lucas?!"

"What?!"

"Dad..." April groaned, seeing her father standing in the doorway.

"Sexual assault? When? Who? And a baby?"

April brought her uninjured hand up to her face. She sniffled once, but could not control the eruption of pent-up emotions that consumed her now. She burst into deep sobs.

"I wondered why you went to Desert Sands Junior year." Trina went to April and held her. The two cried together.

Detective Ramirez motioned for a stunned Mr. Richards to join him and Clark outside.

"Why don't I know about this?"

"I can't answer that. I can tell you that April is going to need you to be strong for her. Standing up to your attackers is not a simple thing to do."

"Yes, of course. Did they all...?"

"From our understanding, it was two of them."

"The same two that...?" Mr. Richards motioned to his daughter's room.

"Yes."

"I hope they get..." Mr. Richards trailed off, his voice breaking as he slumped to the floor. He ran a hand through his hair in frustration. "She's been through so much, and I couldn't ... I couldn't even protect her."

Clark cleared his throat and then kneeled down next to Mr. Richards. "You're not responsible for their wrongdoings." He patted Mr. Richards' arm and then stood.

"Be there for her in the coming months. Testify to what you witnessed in court. They will get their due punishment; I promise you that." Detective Ramirez helped Mr. Richards to his feet.

"Thank you." Mr. Richards strode toward his daughter's hospital room.

And when the time came, April had her day in court...

"Mrs. Altman, call your first witness."

"Thank you, Your Honor. The prosecution calls April Richards."

April approached the witness stand, her eyes scanning the floor beneath her feet. After swearing the oath, she cleared her throat, sniffled, and then sat down.

"Ms. Richards, how were your school years?"

April exhaled hard. "It was horrible. I hated having to go to school."

"Why is that?"

"There was a group of boys that bullied me, terrorized really, for most of my school years."

"Do you see any of them in the courtroom today?"

"Yes." April's hand trembled as she pointed towards the table where Wes and Adam sat. "The defendants are two of them."

"I'd like to skip forward to the night of August seventh 2011."

April clamped her eyes shut and swallowed hard.

"Can you explain the events for the court?"

"I was staying with my friend, Kylan Best. A mutual friend had invited us to a house party."

"Were you and Mr. Best dating?"

"No. We were friends. At least I thought we were." April bit her bottom lip, recalling that night in her head.

"I don't really want to go, Kylan."

Taking her book, he placed it on the table, and then unclipped the barrette from her hair. "Let your hair down. You study all the time. Your grades are fantastic. If you don't have fun once in a while, you'll go crazy..."

"I have fun."

"What's the last fun thing you've done?"

"I ... went to dinner with my dad a couple nights ago."

"Outings with parents don't count. Come on. Give it an hour. If you hate it after that, we can leave."

April held up her index finger. "One hour."

Kylan smiled.

The music was loud as the pair entered the house. People danced, laughed, and talked as far as April could see.

"Let's go find Christopher."

"What?"

Kylan laughed, taking April's hand. "Come on."

They made their way through the wall-to-wall people and ended up in the kitchen.

"I didn't see him."

"In the midst of all this chaos, how could you?" April motioned to the crowd.

"I bet he's playing Immortals and Legends."

"While his party is going on?" April raised her brow. "Yeah, he probably is."

"I'm going to get him."

"You better not leave me to play video games."

"No, no. I'll be right back. I promise."

April waited five, ten, and finally fifteen minutes for Kylan to return. She sighed. "I never leave the house without a book in my bag." April pulled out a chair and sat down. She removed a book from her bag, opened it, and read.

"The good stuff is always in the kitchen."

April turned around at the voice.

"I didn't expect to find you here."

April groaned, shutting the book. "Just who I didn't want to see."

"Aw, don't be like that."

"Yeah, we're at a party. "

"Whoopie." April rolled her eyes, twirling a finger in the air.

"If you're not having fun, why are you here?"

"Christopher invited us."

"Us?" Adam scanned the room. "You're a bit old for imaginary friends."

April let out her best fake laugh. "I'm here with Kylan."

"Where's Mr. Love Sick Puppy?"

"We're just friends."

"Mm hmm, someone should tell him that."

"It isn't like that."

Wes held up his hands in mock surrender. "Okay, whatever you say."

"Well, since Kylan has left you all alone, how about you have a drink with us?" Adam held out a plastic cup.

"No, thanks."

"What, you're too good for us?"

"I wouldn't hang out with you two if you were the last guys on earth."

"Now that's just rude."

"Don't pretend we are friends. I get enough of your shit at school. I don't need it outside of it too." April crammed her book into her bag before storming out of the room and making her way up the stairs. She went to the room at the end of the hall, opening the door. Sitting on the floor, she took the book back out to read.

She made it through two chapters when the door opened.

"Someone's in here."

"We meet again." Adam laughed.

"We keep bumping into each other." Wes swayed.

"Wonderful." April put her book back into her bag and stood. "Have you two been drinking?"

"*We ARE at a party.*"

April sighed and picked up her bag. She strode across the room toward the door.

"You're leaving already?"

"Yeah, you ruined the only quiet spot I found in the house. I'll just call Trina to come get me."

Adam grabbed her arm, jerking her backward. She stumbled back, landing on Christopher's bed.

"Freaking jerk." April tried to stand, but Adam and Wes blocked her path.

"You need to learn to lighten up."

"Get out of my way!"

"Shh, let's have our own little party." Wes straddled April.

She thrashed, crying out for help.

Adam jumped on the bed beside her, clamping his hand over her mouth. "Shut up!"

Wes captured her arms in one hand, raising them over her head, while using the other hand to unbutton her pants. April's screams were muffled by the boys' rough hands as they took turns having their way with her.

April broke down on the stand, sobbing inconsolably, her hand covering her face.

"Your honor, I request a short recess."

"Granted. We'll convene in thirty minutes."

Chapter 6

"Are you able to continue, Ms. Richards?"

"Yes, Your Honor. Thank you for the time to ... compose myself."

"What was your life like after the assault?"

"I hardly left the house. I took online classes my junior year."

"Was there another reason besides fear that prompted your transfer to an online school that year?"

"Yes. A few months after ... after that night, I found out I was pregnant."

"And you had the baby?"

"I did. I couldn't have an abortion. It wasn't his fault the way he..."

"He? You had a boy?"

"Yes. Lucas Richards."

"Your Honor, I'd like to call your attention to exhibit A." Mrs. Altman strolled from the table to the witness stand, handing a piece of paper to April. "Ms. Richards, could you tell the court what that document is?"

"It's Lucas' birth certificate."

"What is the date listed on the certificate?"

"May thirteenth, 2012."

"And who is listed as mother?"

"April Richards."

"And under father?"

"Unknown."

"I would like to call attention to exhibit B." Mrs. Altman took Lucas's birth certificate from April, handing her another piece of paper. "What is this document?"

"It's Lucas's..." April sniffled. "His death certificate."

"What did they list as a cause of death, Ms. Richards?"

"Natural causes/ SIDS."

"What is the date on the document?"

"June seventeenth, 2012." April sniffled.

"I'm very sorry for your loss, Ms. Richards."

"Th ... thank you."

"I would like to fast forward to January twenty-third of this year. Can you describe for the court the events of that day?"

"My last class was over at noon. After that, I went to see my friend Jonathan Jones. I had dinner plans with my father that night, but I never made it to the restaurant."

"Why?"

"On my way home, I noticed a car following me."

"What did you do?"

I stopped at the gas station, wanting to make sure my paranoia wasn't getting the best of me. I phoned my roommate, filling her in on my encounter with Adam Jones when I was at his brother's house.

"What type of run in?"

April vividly described her verbal altercation with Adam.

"What happened next?"

"I got in my car to go home. While driving, a car ran me off the road. The two defendants exited their vehicle, walking toward my car."

"What did you do?"

"My car wouldn't start, so I climbed over the seat, out of the passenger side. I sprinted into the woods. Something caused me to stumble; I hit the ground. I screamed. Adam said, 'Get back here'..."

"I was out of it for a while. I finally pulled my phone from my pocket to call Trina ... My roommate. We have a 'find my phone' app. When she saw me, she started asking questions. I remember saying 'bullies', then I must have passed out. I don't remember anything after that until I woke up in the hospital."

"Thank you, April. No further questions, Your Honor."

"Does the defense wish to cross-examine?"

Adam and Wes's lawyer stood, straightening his tie before picking up a leather clipboard off the table. As he was about to step forward,

Wes's hand shot out and grabbed his arm, tears running down his face. "Enough."

Adam smacked Wes' hand. "What are you doing?"

Wes stood. "What I should have done from the beginning."

Wes's revelations stopped any further proceedings. April barely heard the judge say she could step down. Once that registered, all April wanted was to escape. His words still rang in April's ears as she ran out of the courtroom, down the hall, and out the front door.

After all this time, the countless denials of wrongdoing, the years of torturing her, why choose now to do the right thing? There was no way she misjudged his character. From childhood to young adult, he was an active participant in the abuse heaped on her. He was there that night. He did that horrible thing, took something from her she could never get back. A girl's purity was all she had to take pride in; her honor and decency in a world that wasn't always so meant something. And then to lose Lucas was like pouring a bag of salt into a gaping wound.

The tears and snot ran down her face. She plopped down on the corner of the front steps, fresh rain soaking through her skirt, though she hardly felt it. A warm hand touched her shoulder. A sniffle, and then she was in her best friend's arms.

"I'm here."

April buried her face into Trina's shoulder. Deep sobs escaped; she took solace from the girl that had always been her rock, her savior from the torture of four boys that, for whatever reason, had made it their goal to destroy her joy in life.

Trina sat April straight up to face her. "I would fight the world for you, you know."

April sniffled, nodding.

A handkerchief slipped over her left shoulder, a whiff of her dad's aftershave drifting with it. She took the hanky. Soon the cool breeze stopped, blocked by her father sitting protectively behind her.

"Never, my girl. You will never again have to ..." Her father's words trailed off. She found her hand in his.

"I'm sorry."

"My God, kid, what for? You did nothing wrong. If anything, I should have fought harder to protect you."

"What happens now?"

"Justice, April. Justice."

"I don't think I can face him."

"You don't have to. Wes admitted everything. The trial is over."

"Not him."

Trina and April's father shared a glance.

April took a ragged breath.

Trina gave her hand a squeeze. "If it comes to it, we will face it together."

"The three of us," her father added.

"The prosecution and defense have reached a plea agreement?"

"Yes, Your Honor."

"It says here under the terms of this deal Mr. Best will testify in another trial?"

"Yes, Your Honor."

"Before I continue with sentencing, I have a question. What are the details surrounding the intent to commit charge?"

Kylan glanced at his lawyer and then around the room.

"Mr. Best?"

Kylan snapped his head up toward the judge. "Your Honor."

"The details."

"I ... uh—"

Kylan's lawyer motioned for him to stand.

Kylan stood. "I was only going to talk to her."

"That is not intent to commit a crime."

"Exactly. That is what I've been saying. It's not my fault she stopped talking to me. I mean, she accepted Trevor's invitation to the party. Why did she tell me no when I asked her out? She can only expect me to put up with the disrespect for so long."

Kylan's lawyer made motions for Kylan to stop talking.

The judge's eyebrow rose.

Kylan continued his rambling. "I gave her a place to stay, keeping the bullies away. What right did she have to treat me like I was beneath her? Yes, I followed her that day. Who wouldn't! I was only going to scare her, maybe give back some of the hurt she caused. Not much, just … enough. Yeah, just…"

Kylan's lawyer tugged at Kylan's suit jacket to get him to stop, but his efforts were in vain. Kylan had gone over the edge. He was no longer lying about being sick.

"But they got there first! I followed them into the woods. Her screams were music to my ears…"

Kylan's lawyer stood, glancing at Kylan once, and then clearing his throat. "Your Honor, clearly the defendant needs a few moments to—"

"Clearly, Mr. Best needs more help than a few minutes can provide. I cannot in good conscious honor the plea agreement."

"Yes, just one more kick. Another … the blood. It splattered on the ground!"

"Bailiff, remove the defendant from my courtroom!"

Kylan continued his babbling as the bailiff led him from the room.

His lawyer slumped back down in his seat.

"The defendant will be held without bail pending psychological examination."

"Yes, Your Honor."

Clark strode through the door of his office and handed Ramirez a cup of coffee. "I'd call that a win, Ramirez."

"It will be an extremely long time until Wes and Adam see the light of day."

Clark nodded. "And Kylan won't see the outside of Spring Forest until he's gray and wrinkled."

"Maybe not even then. I heard they had to sedate him to shut him up."

"Wes's confession was a shocker."

"Crushed under the weight of guilt?"

"You saw his face go pale when he heard about Lucas."

"It goes to show you that even the worst of people can do the right thing."

"I just hope April can find peace and move on from all of this."

"She has two good friends and a supportive father."

"And she is stronger than she even realizes."

"Hey, April!"

April clutched her books to her body, turning around. She took a deep breath, straightening her spine, head held high.

"Want to get coffee before class?"

April's face lit up.

Trina giggled, giving John's hand a squeeze.

They hugged her, taking turns. April strode forward with Trina on her left and John on her right. They laughed, collecting their morning brew on the way to class.

With each day, April's life got a little easier. The torment from her past, not forgotten, settled into the back of her mind. With support from her father and friends, she continued to thrive, her loathing turning into hope.

Also by Sharon Lopez

My Right to Choose
Dillon

Sanguisuge
Sanguisuge
Sanguisuge Book 2
Sanguisuge Book 3
Sanguisuge Book 4
Sanguisuge Book 5
Sanguisuge book 6

Stephanie
The World Inside Stephanie's Head
The World Beyond Stephanie's Head
The Stephanie Series

The Mark
Destiny's Mark

Before the Mark
The Mark Series

Standalone
Life is Funny That Way
Alright, Well I Love You
The Problem with Emma
Emotions Behind the Chaos
My Right To Choose
Embracing Vengeance
From a God to The Puppeteer
April's Showers

Watch for more at azteddie.wix.com/sharon-lopez.

About the Author

Sharon is a multi-genre young adult author that dabbles in adult tales from time to time. It's all about the story is not just a catchphrase but a spirit that is inside all of her books. When she is not writing, she can be found getting lost in other author's worlds, watching Slice Of Life Anime, or getting annihilated as she tries her hand at various video games.

She is inspired by many things. Whether it's an encouraging word, a kooky dream, or a personal experience, she will put it to excellent use. As a defender of the defenseless, Sharon's characters take on this persona with strong female leads and males that are protective, perfect, boyfriend material.

Read more at azteddie.wix.com/sharon-lopez.

Milton Keynes UK
Ingram Content Group UK Ltd.
UKHW050635150424
441175UK00013B/479